Martha and Skits Out West

Adaptation by Jamie White
Based on the TV series teleplays written by
Dietrich Smith and Raye Lankford
Based on characters created by Susan Meddaugh

HOUGHTON MIFFLIN HARCOURT
Boston · New York · 2011

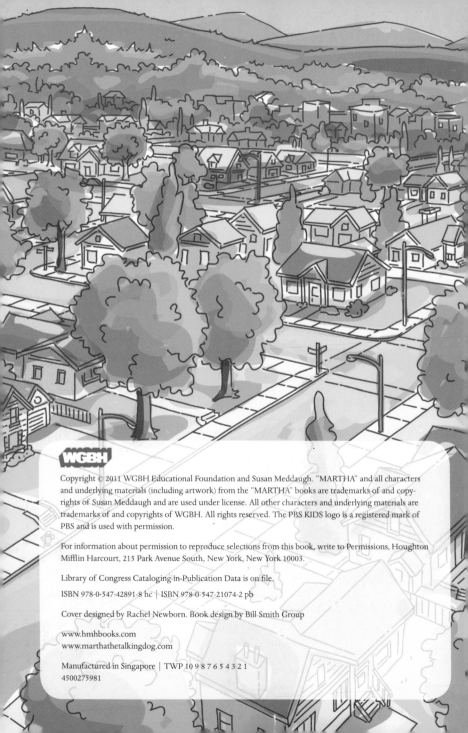

For information about permission to reproduce selections from this book, write to Permissions, Houghton Mifflin Harcourt, 215 Park Avenue South, New York, New York 10003.

Library of Congress Cataloging-in-Publication Data is on file.

ISBN 978-0-547-42891-8 hc | ISBN 978-0-547-21074-2 pb

Cover designed by Rachel Newborn. Book design by Bill Smith Group

www.hmhbooks.com
www.marthathetalkingdog.com

Manufactured in Singapore | TWP 10 9 8 7 6 5 4 3 2 1
4500275981

MARTHA SAYS HOWDY

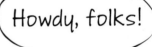

It's me, Martha, back from my family vacation in Montana. Skits and I lived like real cowdogs. Yee-haw!

Okay, maybe I did get us into a heap of trouble out west. But that can happen when you're a rootin' tootin' talkin' dog.

1

Ever since Helen fed me her alphabet soup, I've been able to speak. And speak and speak . . . No one's sure how or why, but the letters in the soup traveled up to my brain instead of down to my stomach.

Now as long as I eat my daily bowl of alphabet soup, I can talk. To my family—Helen, baby Jake, Mom, Dad, and Skits, who only speaks Dog. To Helen's friends—T.D., Truman, and Alice. To anyone who'll listen.

My speaking comes in handy, too. One night I called 911 to stop a burglar!

Sometimes my family wishes I didn't talk *quite* so much. But they love having me around. So they were disappointed when I first said I didn't want to travel with them.

Just ask Dad.

We were getting suitcases from the attic for the summer family vacation. Well, Dad got them. I gave myself the important job of sniffing them. I started with the green suitcase. It smelled like plastic leis and a hint of the ocean. Ahh!

"Where did this one come from?" I asked.

Dad read the tag. "We used that suitcase on our trip to Hawaii last summer."

I sniffed a blue suitcase. Mmm, beef taco. "And this one?"

"Mom took that one to Mexico," Dad said.

Last came the brown suitcase. I gave it a whiff. Leather, mothballs, and . . . yes, fish and chips!

"Grandma and Granddad borrowed that one for their trip to England," said Dad.

"I like Mexico the best," I decided.

"It is nice." Dad sighed happily.

I imagined the beautiful scenery. Tasty bones, fish heads, mysterious rotting things . . . And that's just the *Mexican* garbage cans. I could visit the tropical trash of Hawaii and the rain-soaked rubbish of England, too. Why, I'd have my own worldwide trash tour!

"I wish I could travel with you guys," I said.

"So do we, old girl," said Dad.

But as much as I longed to go with my family, the thought of flying made me more scared than a cat in a dog show.

So how did I end up out west?

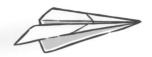

TWO HORRIBLE WORDS

Hot dog, chewy, toilet . . . I have many favorite words. But there are two words I *cannot* say. (Well, maybe for a Burger Barn triple-bacon cheeseburger.)

Of course, they were bound to come up when Helen and her friends—T.D., Truman, and Alice—shared their summer plans as they folded paper airplanes.

"We're going camping," said Helen's best friend, T.D. "What about you guys?"

Nowheresville, I thought with a sigh.

"Montana," said Helen, tossing her plane. "Dude ranch."

Without me, I thought, sighing louder.

"Grandma's taking me to Washington, D.C., to see the museums," said Truman.

Will I be the only one left in Wagstaff City?

"We're going to Aspen," said Alice, rolling her eyes. *"Again."*

Alice clumsily threw her plane. Being Alice's plane, it looped back and crashed into her ear. "Ow!" she cried. With all those mountains to trip over, I could see why Alice might want to give Aspen a skip.

"If only *I* could travel," I said.

"Why can't you?" asked Alice. "Dogs can go on planes, right?"

"She can," said Helen. "Skits
is going to Montana with us."

"He's going with you, yes. But he's not
going *with* you," I said.

T.D. looked confused. "I don't get it."

"Two words . . . but I can't say them," I said.

"Cargo hold," Helen said for me.

I shuddered at those two terrifying words.

"Cargo hold? What's that?" asked Alice.

I flipped a paper airplane upside down with my nose. "That," I said, eyeing it.

Helen explained. "Cargo is the stuff a plane or ship carries. Like the crates, boxes, and suitcases. The cargo hold is a space in the bottom of the plane where the cargo is stored."

"And that's where the dogs go," I said.

"In a *suitcase?*" asked Alice, throwing another plane. This one looped back to crash into T.D.'s ear.

"Ow!" he yelped. (It was always risky to sit near Alice.)

"No, in a *cage*," I said. "In the *dark*. In the *bottom of the plane*."

I told them how an evil baggage handler would toss me into the plane. I'd tumble to the bottom of a dark, creepy staircase. There I'd stay, trapped in a flying doggy dungeon! "Otherwise known as *the cargo hold*," I said.

"It can't be that bad," said Truman.

"How do you know? Have *you* ever been in a cargo hold?"

"No. Have you?"

"Er . . . no," I mumbled.

"So how do you know what it's like if you haven't tried it?" asked Truman.

"How do you know what a volcano is like if you haven't jumped into one?" I replied.

Truman nodded. "She's got a point."

Meanwhile, Alice had finished another plane. "That ought to do it," she said, throwing it.

"AAAAAH!" we shouted, ducking.

But her plane flew without poking a single ear.

I admired Alice's paper airplane. But one thing was for sure. I was not stepping one paw onto a real one.

FLYING LESSONS AT THE FIRE HYDRANT

Yup, it was true. My family was going to Montana . . . *without* me!

If only dogs didn't have to go in the cargo hold. So much for being man's best friend.

From the hallway, I watched Dad in his room, packing and yakking on the phone.

"I'll drop Jake off in an hour, Mom," he said, hanging up. Dad looked frazzled. Suddenly he looked around, alarmed. "Where *is* Jake? Did I pack him?"

Jake giggled. Dad was so busy, he forgot he
had picked him up after setting the clothes down.

"Never mind," said Dad, smiling.

Someone needed a vacation.

I wandered over to Helen's room. She was
showing Skits a brochure.

"That's the Montana prairie," she said, pointing to a photo. "It's so huge, you can run as much as you want. It'll be fun!"

As I watched, Mom walked past me.

"Oh, Martha," she said, stopping. "I forgot to tell you about the dogsitter. Lucy had to cancel, so they're sending over a new one tomorrow. His name is Mr. McGrump."

Gah! While my family was whooping it up out west, I'd be stuck with a grumpy McGrump.

I decided to meet my pals at the fire hydrant for some cheering up.

"Hey, guys!" I called. "You know I've been moaning about not going to Montana, but I think I might like staying home. I'll have the whole house to myself! And uh . . . you guys! And . . . the old fire hydrant! Ahh!

"It smells . . ." I gave it a good sniff.

"The same as always," I said, frowning. This wasn't going so well. "Say," I said to the group that had gathered, "have any of you ever gone on a plane before?"

Arf! Yip! Woof, woof. Grr.

"You *all* have? In the cargo hold? What was it like?"

The dogs grunted.

"How could you not know?" I asked. "Were you *asleep?*"

They nodded.

"You *were* asleep? How did you ever sleep through something so scary?"

I couldn't believe what my friends said next.

"Why didn't anyone *tell* me there's a pill dogs take to sleep through the flight?" I asked. Flying was going to be a cinch!

Or so I thought.

MARTHA'S TRAVEL TIP #1

"I'm glad you changed your mind," Helen told me at the airport.

"Me, too," I said.

The airport sure was a busy place. It was full of people. And dogs. And hot dogs, too! (My nose finds snacks anywhere.)

"There are a lot of passengers, huh?" said Helen.

"Are passengers a kind of snack?" I asked hopefully.

"No. Passengers are people traveling on
a plane—or in a train, boat, car, or however
they're traveling."

While Dad checked in at the ticket counter,
we waited. Behind us, a fat gray cat lounged
in her fancy carrier.

Meoooow.

"Oh, yes. We're on the flight to Montana, too," I answered her.

Meow, meow.

"Well, of course I'm taking a pill! Aren't you?"

The cat shook her head.

"You *aren't?*"

Mew, mew, she mocked.

"I am *not* a scaredy-dog!" I said. "Right, Skits?"

Skits didn't reply. Dad had returned and was feeding him a pill wrapped in cheese.

"Your turn, Martha," said Mom, holding open my carrier door.

I walked inside. Helen offered me a pill. I looked at the pill. I looked at the cat.

Meeooow, the cat snickered.

"You know what?" I said. "I'm not going to take a pill."

My family gasped. "WHAT?"

"If that cat's not taking it, *I'm* certainly not." *Take that, cat.* "It'll be exciting to find out what the cargo hold is like," I said, trying to be brave. "I'll be the first dog to stay awake for it."

"But it might be scary when the plane takes off and lands," said Helen gently. "And sometimes there's turbulence. That's when the wind blows and makes the plane shake."

Gulp! That did seem scary.

"Well, turbulence sounds like . . . fun," I said, stretching the truth. "Just wait until that cat sees me again in the cargo hold. I'll be wide awake. Right, Skits?"

Zzzz. Skits snored. (Honestly! He was no help at all.)

Dad placed our carriers onto a conveyer belt. No turning back now. Helen walked beside me as I headed toward a small door.

That's when I spotted . . . *the cat*. Who was definitely NOT going into the cargo hold! She was still with her owner.

"Wait!" I said to Helen. "Why isn't that cat being put on the conveyer belt?"

"Sometimes small animals like cats can ride with their owners in the main cabin," she said.

The cat stuck out her tongue.

"Cats," I muttered, before disappearing into the great unknown. "I could have guessed."

And so you've learned my first travel tip: *Never trust a cat.*

MARTHA LENDS A PAW

"In you go!" said the baggage handler, placing my cage on another conveyer belt.

Up, up I went into the cargo hold.

The plane door slammed shut. In the darkness, I listened to the other dogs snore. I felt alone. And scared.

"Oh, Martha," I said. "Why didn't you take that pill?"

The plane rumbled. Suitcases and cages rattled around me.

"Wha-at's go-ing on?" I wondered aloud.

Then I remembered what Helen had said in the car: "First, the plane moves down the runway. It's called taxiing. Then the plane takes off."

"Ok-kay. It's ju-ust ta-axiing," I said, trying to calm myself down.

The plane's engine roared. The room tilted as the plane took off. My cage slid across the floor.

WHOA!

When the plane straightened again, I came to a stop. We must be in the air. I was flying!

"That's better," I said, settling down. "Now I'll try to sleep *without a pill.*"

I shut my eyes. But all I could see was that cat in her own comfy seat. *She's probably being served cream in a crystal bowl,* I thought. *I didn't even get a lousy peanut!*

My eyes snapped open. Ugh! I wasn't going to fall asleep that way.

Just then, I heard a *creak!* A tall shadow crept across the wall.

Scuffle, scuffle, bump.

Yikes! Who was there? I couldn't wait to tell Truman I was right. It *was* scary in there! I covered my face with my paws. "Go to sleep, Martha. Go to sleep, go to—"

Arf!

I raised my head. Could it be that another dog was awake like I was?

"Are you okay?" I said loudly. A dog whimpered. "Hold on. I'll find you!"

I tried to unlock my carrier door with my paws. No luck. It was too hard to push.

Why, oh why, can't dogs have hands? With my teeth, I pulled on a suitcase tag. Its string stretched against my carrier's unlock button, almost pressing it down.

I pulled and pulled and . . . *SNAP!* The tag sprang back. Its suitcase popped open and toppled a birdcage . . . that hit another suitcase . . . that bounced off a harp.

"Uh-oh!" I said, watching the suitcase whiz across the room.

CRASH! It landed on a box. Out bounced hundreds of rubber balls. In any other situation I would have enjoyed that.

Boing, boing, boing!

The balls bounced past my carrier, when—*boing!*—one bounced right onto the unlock button. *Click!* My door sprang open.

"Yes!" I cried, escaping. "I'm coming!"

I sniffed my way to an open carrier. The lock on the door was broken. Then I found a sleeping pill and saw a small brown dog cringing between some suitcases.

"Ah! You spit out your pill. I bet you won't do *that* again."

The small dog continued to tremble.

"Don't be scared," I said softly. "Riding in the cargo hold is simple. You depart from the airport, fly a few hours, and then arrive where you're going. Soon we'll land at the airport in Montana and be just fine."

The dog was calming down. Unfortunately, that's when the plane began to shake. Suitcases crashed to the floor. The noise woke other dogs from their slumber.

CRASH! BANG! WOOF!

Now the little dog yelped. He was trembling in fear again.

This must be the shaking Helen had warned me about!

"It's okay, everybody," I told the petrified pooches. "This is just turbulence. It's when the wind blows the plane a little. It feels like a bumpy road, right?"

The dogs nodded.

"Nothing to be afraid of. It'll end in a—"

And just as quickly as it began, the shaking stopped.

The dogs relaxed.

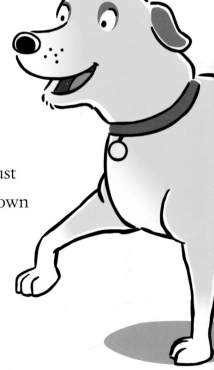

"See?" I said. "No big woof. You can all go back to sleep."

They yawned and did just that. Then I helped the brown dog back into his crate.

When the plane landed in Montana, all was back to normal. (Well, if a talking dog standing on a mountain of suitcases is normal. The baggage handlers didn't look so sure.)

"Hi, guys," I greeted them. "That turbulence made a mess, but don't worry. I cleaned it up for you."

A sleepy-eyed Skits and I met our family in the airport.

"You weren't scared at all?" Helen asked me.

"Not really," I said. "I'll have a lot to tell the gang at the fire hydrant!"

Behind us came a loud *YOWL!*
Who was so hot under the collar?
I turned to see the pilot
holding out a wild gray ball
of fur. I recognized that
ball of fur at once. *The cat.*

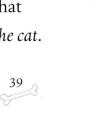

39

"That cat freaked out as soon as the plane took off," Helen said.

"She broke out of her cage," said Mom. "The crew chased her around the whole flight."

I had to laugh. "You'd never catch a dog doing that!"

THE STRANGERS

It was like a scene out of an old Western . . .

On a dusty road, two cowboys faced the gang of strangers who'd just hit town.

Tumbleweeds rolled. A snake rattled and hissed.

The tough old cowboy cast a fretful glance at his partner.

"This looks bad, Slim," said the old cowboy, Cookie.

Slim, tall and silent, nodded as the strangers stepped closer.

It was bad, all right. The strangers—a little red-haired girl, her parents, and two dogs—looked like city folk. Cookie doubted they'd ever seen a real horse, let alone ridden one.

"Howdy, cowboys!" said one of the dogs. "I'm Martha!"

"AAAH!" Cookie yelled, leaping into Slim's arms. "What in tarnation?"

I had a feeling that Cookie and Slim, our dude ranch guides, had never met a talking dog before.

Once Cookie got over his shock, he ordered us into his old school-bus-turned-tour bus. My family sat nervously as Cookie drove.

"I guess I forgot to mention in my e-mail that Martha speaks," said Dad.

Cookie scowled. "Ain't fittin'."

"Why are we going to a ranch, anyway?" I asked. "I thought on vacation, people stayed in hotels."

Dad grinned. "Not on this vacation. We're going on a cattle drive."

"Driving cows? Wow!" I said. "Western cows must be talented. And tiny. Most cows can't even fit into a car, much less drive one."

Helen giggled. "On a cattle drive, the cows don't drive you. You drive them."

Driving a bus full of cows sounded even better. Imagine the sing-alongs! I bet cows love "One hundred bottles of milk on the wall . . ."

The bus arrived at the Lazy 8 Ranch, where
the cows greeted us from behind a fence.
Mooo!

"I think we need a bigger bus," I said.
Those cows would *never* fit through the door.

"Cattle drives don't have anything to do with cars or buses," said Helen.

"They don't?"

Helen opened her brochure. She pointed to a photo of Slim leading the cows.

"In a cattle drive, people walk cows along a trail, from one ranch to another," Dad said.

He must be joking! "Walking cows?" I asked him. "That's your idea of a vacation?"

"Pretty neat, huh? The great outdoors!" said Dad, throwing out his arms.

"No wonder Jakey stayed home with Grandma Lucille," I whispered to Skits.

Cookie knelt beside me. "On a vacation, you take off work and relax, don't ya?" he said kindly. "Maybe go to the mountains to ski, or to the beach to swim."

"Yes!" I said, getting ready to kick up my paws. "Let's relax and—"

"WELL, THIS AIN'T THAT KIND OF VACATION!" Cookie hollered, leaping up. "It's a cattle drive. Ain't no relaxing or swimming. It's hard work! AND DON'T YOU FORGET IT!"

He stomped off. " 'I want a vacation,' " he mimicked. "City folk!"

"Looks like we got off on the wrong foot with Cookie," Mom said quietly.

"I didn't stand on his feet!" I said. "Either of them."

Mom laughed. "It's an expression. When you say you got off on the wrong foot with someone, it means you made a bad first impression."

I hoped we'd get on the right foot. Soon.

MARTHA'S TRAVEL TIP #2

To turn a dude ranch into a food ranch, find the chuck wagon.

I learned this tip during our first dinner at camp.

"Come and git it!" Cookie yelled, banging a ladle on a pot hanging over the fire.

Clang, clang, clang!

We lined up.

"What's that?" I asked about a funny-looking thing parked nearby. It looked like a tent on wheels.

"It's the chuck wagon," said Helen. "It's where cowboys keep their food on cattle drives."

Skits and I sniffed happily. A chuck wagon was our kind of wagon.

Slim walked past us with his dinner. He took one bite and spat it out. "These vittles ain't fit for a dog," he said, flinging his stew to the ground.

Skits and I rushed to lap it up.

"Au contraire!" I said, licking my lips.

When Cookie wasn't looking, Mom, Dad, and Helen generously gave us their dinner, too. And to think I was worried I wouldn't like this vacation!

"We'll camp here," said Cookie. "Get some shuteye. We'll depart mighty early in the morning." He handed out three sleeping bags.

"Where are we supposed to sleep?" I asked.

"Yer lookin' at it," said Cookie, pointing to the ground.

I pawed the hard dirt. "Outdoors?"

"What's the matter, little doggy?" Cookie asked sweetly. "Maybe you'd like better lodging? You know, a place you stay when you're away from home?"

"That would be great," I said. "Nothing fancy. Maybe just a comfy chair and a—"

"WELL, THERE AIN'T NO LODGING!"
Cookie hollered. "This ain't that kind of
vacation. This is a cattle drive. On a cattle
drive, cowboys camp outdoors. Got it?"

We quickly nodded. "Yessir!" "Uh-huh!"
"Got it!" *Woof!*

Cookie stomped off, muttering, "City folk."

Now I'd done it. I had stepped on his other
wrong foot.

MOOOOVE 'EM OUT

The next morning, it was time for the cattle drive. From all Cookie's jabbering about work, I expected something harder than trotting alongside a bunch of slowpoke cows.

"This is work?" I said to Skits as we ran. "Ha! I could do this all day!"

We ran.

And ran.

And ran some more.

"Er, maybe this is a little work," I said, panting.

"Martha, would you like to ride up here with me?" Dad asked.

"*Would* I?" I said. I scrambled onto Dad's saddle. "Wow! You can see far up here."

The prairie spread out in all directions. It was like the world's biggest doggy park.

"Makes you feel like a real cowboy, doesn't it?" said Dad. He was so happy, he began to sing. "*Whoop-ee ti-yi-yo, git along, little dogies!*"

"Hey!" I snapped. "What's the idea? 'Git along, dogie'? You invited me up here."

"You're not a dogie. You're a doggy. A dogie is a motherless cow."

"That's not a very nice song," I said. "First the baby cow loses its mother. Then you tell it to get lost. The words ought to be more inviting. Like this:

Whoop-ee ti-yi-yo, have a seat, little dogies.
I know your mama don't want you to roam."

As I sang, a funny thing happened. The cows stopped walking—and had a seat!

Our cattle drive had come to a mooing halt. Those git-along dogies had turned into sit-along dogies.

"Now look what you've done!" Cookie yelled. "This is a cattle drive! Cows can't sit! They're supposed to move along the trail!"

Oops. I tried pushing the cows up from their big behinds. "It was just a song," I pleaded. "When I said, 'have a seat,' I didn't mean it. Let's mooooove 'em out!"

Mooooooooooooo!

"What do you mean, 'Noooooooooooo'?" I asked the cows.

Cookie and Slim looked angrier than bulls chewing bumblebees.

"While the cows are sitting, why don't we do some sightseeing?" Helen suggested. "We can tour around on our horses and look at the scenery."

"Sightseeing?" said Cookie.

"Yes," said Mom. "When you sightsee, you visit the fun things in the place where you're vacationing."

"Don't that sound nice!" said Cookie. "We could take pictures, couldn't we?"

My family nodded. "Yes!" "Great idea!" *Woof!* "Now you're talk—"

"EXCEPT WE'RE NOT DOING NO SIGHTSEEING!" Cookie hollered. "This ain't that kind of vacation. This is a *cattle drive.* There's no taking purdy pictures of scenery. The only sights you'll be seeing is the backside of a cow!"

Suddenly, there was a *click* and flash of light. Cookie swayed, blinded by Dad's camera.

"Uh, sorry," said Dad.

Cookie stumbled away.

"Now I'm on the wrong foot," said Helen.

"Me, too," said Dad.

"Me, too," said Mom.

"Welcome to my world," I said.

MARTHA'S TRAVEL TIP #3

Under a full moon, the cows sat on.

"We'll break camp extra early tomorrow because of the cow sitting today," Cookie grumbled. He stomped off to sleep under the wagon.

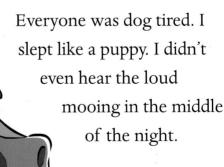

Everyone was dog tired. I slept like a puppy. I didn't even hear the loud mooing in the middle of the night.

But Helen did. She checked the herd. The cows seemed nervous. She tiptoed over to Cookie. He was awake, too.

"Cookie?" she whispered. "Something's wrong with the cows."

"There's wolves out there," he said. "The cows can smell them. They make the cows jumpy."

In the distance, a wolf howled. The familiar sound jolted me awake.

"Kinfolk!" I exclaimed. I answered back with a *HOOOOWL!*

And that's how I discovered travel tip #3: *Never howl in the company of cows.*

If hearing a distant wolf makes cows jumpy, hearing a howl in their own camp makes them leap clear off their hooves.

"STAMPEDE!" yelled Cookie, scooting out from under the wagon. He lifted Helen just before the herd thundered by.

"What's a stampede?" I asked.

"A stampede is when a bunch of animals or people run away because they're scared," said Mom, looking pretty scared herself.

"We've got to stop those cows!" cried Cookie.

The grownups rode off after the cattle while Helen waited safely behind. Skits and I followed on paw.

"Yeeee-haw!" yelled Dad, waving his hat. "Yee-haw!"

"STOP YELLIN' 'YEE-HAW'! " Cookie shouted from his wagon.

"Why?" asked Dad. "I thought that's what cowboys do."

"YES, WHEN WE WANT THE COWS TO MOVE! WE WANT 'EM TO STAY PUT!"

The cows ran on and on. Finally, Slim
caught up to the head of the herd. At the
wave of his hat, the cows turned and stopped.

"Hooray! You did it!" I cheered.

Cookie loomed over me. "*You* are lodging
in the wagon tonight!" he ordered.

"Why? What did I do?" I asked.

He picked me up and dumped me in the back of the wagon. "Howled like a wolf around a cow, that's what."

"I won't talk like a wolf ever again! I promise!"

But Cookie was already shutting the wagon's doors.

"Shouldn't be talkin' at all," he grumbled. "Ain't fittin'."

A CLIFFHANGER

I didn't see anyone again until the next morning, when Cookie opened the wagon's doors.

"Soon as we eat breakfast," he said to Helen, "we'll break camp and—*what?*"

At the sight of me, Cookie's jaw dropped. Helen gasped. Skits whimpered. And I, er . . . burped.

It had been a good night. With a big belly to prove it, I sprawled among bones and empty boxes.

"Martha!" said Helen. "You ate all the food in the chuck wagon!"

"I did not," I said. "There are still some . . . cans of beans left."

Skits sniffed one.

"I couldn't figure out how to work the can opener," I whispered to him.

No one was happy with me. Not even the cows. After a bean breakfast, we trudged along in the hot sun. Skits and I walked alongside Helen's horse—far away from the herd.

"Why can't I walk with the cows?" I asked Helen. "I won't make them stampede again! Honest. I've learned my lesson!"

But Cookie wasn't taking any chances. That night, he tied me to a stake in the ground.

"You're the worst cattle dog I've ever seen," he said.

"I know," I agreed sadly. "You won't hear another word out of me."

From their sleeping bags, my family watched Cookie stomp off to bed.

"You're sure Martha will be all right?" Helen asked. "I can't stand to see her camp all by herself."

"Cookie thinks it's best for the cows," said Mom.

Skits padded over to keep me company, and we soon fell asleep.

But something woke me up. I sniffed the air. I smelled rain. Sure enough, the sky rumbled. Skits huddled by my side.

"I know, Skits. I hear it, too. Sounds like a thunderstorm."

CRACK! Lightning flashed across the sky. Slim and Cookie jumped to their feet. But the spooked cattle were already off.

"Holy cow! Another stampede!" I exclaimed.
"At least it's not my fault this time."

CRACK! A second bolt of lightning made the
horses run, too.

Now we didn't have cows, or horses to help
get the cows. We were stuck. And that wasn't
the worst of it.

"The cattle are going to run right over the cliff!" cried Cookie, pointing up ahead. "The cows won't see it. They're blind with fear."

"Skits!" I said. "Help me dig up this stake."

Together, we dug and dug.

Woof? Skits asked me.

"I think I know a way we can stop those cows!"

The stake came free. Skits and I ran for the herd . . .

MARTHA SAYS SO LONG

Now for my plan. I took a deep breath, and sang:

Whoop-ee ti-yi-yo,
have a seat,
little dogies.
I know your
mama don't want
you to roam.

The cows seemed to be listening. But they didn't stop, so I kept on singing. We were nearly out of time!

Cookie and the others ran after us.

"Look!" yelled Cookie. "The cows are slowing down. Everybody! Sing!"

Skits and I raced ahead. We stopped at the edge of the cliff. Facing the herd, I sang as loudly as I could:

"*Whoop-ee ti-yi-yo, rest your feet, little dogies. You know you should make yourself feel right at home.*"

The cows slowed to a trot. We all held our breath as they skidded to the edge of the cliff and . . . had a seat!

"Hooray, Martha and Skits!" everyone cheered.

Even Cookie.

I felt like a real cowdog. Yes, sirree, just call me the Bone Ranger.

The next day, Cookie drove us to the airport.

"Martha, I was wrong about you," he said, patting my head. "You're the best cattle dog this drive has ever seen."

It turns out Cookie really wasn't so mean, after all.

"Now, what are the words to that song again?" he asked.

"Whoop-ee ti-yi-yo!" we sang.

Our voices carried across the range as we rode off into the sunset. Yes, our western adventure had come to an end.

Just like this story.

Now git along, little dogies!

Yeeeeeee-haw!

GLOSSARY

H ow many words do you remember from the story?

arrive: to get someplace

camping: living outdoors

cargo: the stuff carried in a plane, ship, or other vehicle

cattle drive: the walking of cows along a trail from one ranch to another

depart: to leave

lodging: a place to stay when away from home

passenger: someone traveling on a plane, train, boat, car, or other vehicle

scenery: a view of the outdoors

sightseeing: seeing fun sights in the place where one's vacationing

stampede: a bunch of animals or people running away because they're scared

turbulence: the shaking of a plane caused by wind

vacation: a relaxing break from work or school

Hey, buckaroos! Here's another tip for you. On your next vacation, create a **travel journal.** In a notebook, draw a picture of what you do every day, and write about it. Add ticket stubs, brochures, photos, and other moo-mentos.

What to include:

- Destination. Where are you going?
- Traveling companion(s). Who is going with you?
- Cargo. What are you packing? What do your suitcases smell like?
- Dates. When do you arrive and depart?
- Travel. Are you a passenger on a train, ship, or plane? (If there's turbulence, remember it's no big woof.)
- Lodging. Are you camping, staying in a hotel, or sleeping in a doghouse?
- Scenery. While sightseeing, what do you see? (I hope it's garbage! Mmm.)
- Activities. Like what you do, places you visit, and people and pets you meet.

Giddy up! The Lazy 8 Ranch needs your help in rounding up words. How many words can you make from the letters in STAMPEDE? Use a dictionary to check your answers. (For expert cowpokes, try CATTLE DRIVE, too.)

Doggy Dream
Vacation

No vacation planned? No problem. Dream up an adventure with me, Martha! Using your imagination, choose a place you'd like us to visit and then create a travel journal of our trip. (Don't forget my chewy!)